Evincepub Publishing

Evincepub Publishing

Parijat Extension, Bilaspur, Chhattisgarh 495001
First Published by Evincepub Publishing 2021
Copyright © Sabahat Qayoom 2021
All Rights Reserved.
ISBN: 978-93-5446-073-9

This book has been published with all reasonable efforts taken to make the material error-free after the consent of the author. No part of this book shall be used, reproduced in any manner whatsoever without written permission from the author, except in the case of brief quotations embodied in critical articles and reviews. The Author of this book is solely responsible and liable for its content including but not limited to the views, representations, descriptions, statements, information, opinions and references ["Content"]. The Content of this book shall not constitute or be construed or deemed to reflect the opinion or expression of the Publisher or Editor. Neither the Publisher nor Editor endorse or approve the Content of this book or guarantee the reliability, accuracy or completeness of the Content published herein and do not make any representations or warranties of any kind, express or implied, including but not limited to the implied warranties of merchantability, fitness for a particular purpose. The Publisher and Editor shall not be liable whatsoever for any errors, omissions, whether such errors or omissions result from negligence, accident, or any other cause or claims for loss or damages of any kind, including without limitation, indirect or consequential loss or damage arising out of use, inability to use, or about the reliability, accuracy or sufficiency of the information contained in this book.

Don't Die Before Your Death

Sabahat Qayoom

ACKNOWLEDGEMENT

---•---

The world is a better place thanks to people who want to develop it and live for others. What makes it even better are people who share the gift of their time to mentor future of others. Thank you to everyone who strives to grow and help others to grow."

To all the individuals I have had the opportunity to lead, be led by, or watch their leadership, I want to say thank you for being the inspiration and foundation.

Without the experiences and support from my peers and family, this book would not exist. You have given me the opportunity to lead a great group of individuals—to be a leader of great leaders is a blessed place to be. Thank you to Dad, Mom.

Having an idea and turning it into a book is as hard as it sounds. The experience is both internally challenging and rewarding. I especially want to thank the individuals that helped make this happen. Complete thanks to Dad, Mom, Muniba Mazaria, Azhar Yousuf, Dadu (Abdul Gaffar), Junaid-ul-islam.

Allama Iqbal (Name of the person who helped the most), thank you for being a leader I trust, honour, and respect. I will always welcome the chance to represent you. "Thank You"

Allama Iqbal

CONTENT TABLE

---◆---

HARD WORK 1
FAILURES ARE THE PILLARS OF SUCCESS 3
CHARACTER IS DESTINY 6
FACE IS THE INDEX OF MIND 9
HONESTY 11
WHERE THERE IS WILL THERE IS WAY 13
THE PROBLEMS OF UNEMPLOYMENT 14
SCIENCE AND RELIGION 16
MAN IS THE SOCIAL ANIMAL 20
WISDOM IS POWER (STORY) 21
EDUCATION 23
PARENTS ARE THE REAL SUCCESS 24
LIFE 26
EDUCATING GIRL MEANS EDUCATING FAMILY 28
WORK IS WORSHIP 30
A MAN IS KNOWN BY THE COMPANY HE KEEPS 31
As YOU SOW, SO SHALL YOU WILL REAP 32
FROM ADAM (A.S.) TO 21ST CENTURY 33
STORY OF WOMEN 35
FAITH 38
MOTIVATION TO CREATE LIFE 40
SAY 'NO' TO DRUGS 45

OH MY GOD, OH MY GOD, ... 46
ALLAMA IQBAL 49

CHAPTER 1
HARD WORK

"Hard work is not to success it is to be successful" hard work means to put full concentration on giving point. It is not mandatory to read and write for whole day and night. No, if you are studying why that be one minute but do work on that minute. Give 100% towards your talent and do hard work on that so definitely success will kiss your feet. Don't be lazy be withy. You will definitely achieve success marks didn't matters knowledge matters.

If you have knowledge if your concepts are clear and no one can stop you.
Go through group studies you will get experience from one another and that experience leads to success. Everything needs time to make it complete. Be always courageous person and feel encouraged. Hard work will make your dreams alive if you will read, read thoroughly make its copy one your brain.

Those who are yearning to awake, those who are waiting to be lighten, this is real play of life. The real hard worker is who have strong desire, to think deeply, to understand, and have a thirsty of getting success. If you will hard work you will light the world.

You can pull all the negativity from society. Don't run after great wealth or excessive greed but run after success you will be man, sitting at a constant place will not make your future bright. How much you will hard work you will get more success hard work depends upon thirsty of learning but run after success you will be man sitting at a constant place will not make your future bright how much you will hard work you will get more success. Hard work depends upon thirsty of learning. Your parents always told you follow your dreams, follow your desires, do hard work, because they want you to shine.

When you will stay at right path, then you are successful. If you will stay at right path world salute you but in opposite it will lead you bad way. Thinking is the hardest work there is, which is probably the reason so few engage in it.

———◆———

CHAPTER 2

FAILURES ARE THE PILLARS OF SUCCESS

---◆---

Success and failures are two aspects of human life. Sometimes we fail in our efforts. The proverb means success through failures. So failures should not discourage you. Those who fail one should try again and again. When we fail once, we have some experience of failures. We learn by experience in our second attempt. Our experiences makes us wiser. This is the foundation of success. In fact, success depends upon wisdom and self-confidence. We should not take the proverb in the literal meaning. It is wrong to think that the more a man fails, the surer will be his success. The proverb means no such thing. Failures are nothing but failures.

They can have a damaging effect on your life. So we should not try to fail. If at all we fail, the failure should not discourage us but they should make our will stronger to act with greater determination for success. We must know the cause of our failure. Only a fool thinks that success is easy. Confidence is good, but over confidence is bad. Confidence gives us strength. Over confidence makes us easy going. The man who thinks that he is too wiser, and too intelligent may also fail. Some people fail because they get too nervous. They fear failure before it actually happens. Such people are defeated from within. So they are bound to fail.

We must know how to succeed in life. We must have certain mental qualities for that first. We must be hardworking. We have to try again and again for success. Secondly, we should have courage we must have the will power to succeed. We should not accept defeat at any cost. We shall lose the battle of life if we feel defeated. We have to accept the challenge with determination and courage of course, failures upset us at time. But we must have strong spirit and undefeatable desire for victory in life. When we fail we should remember the proverb

"Failures are the pillars of success. There are many examples in history to prove what this proverb say to us. "Failure is not fatal like it can be the stepping stone to success".

CHAPTER 3

CHARACTER IS DESTINY

———•♦•———

A fatalist believe is destiny. According to him fate is prewritten thing. They can't be change or can't make by the human being. Character may be defined as the sum total of qualities that a man possesses. It is the greatest and most powerful factor in human life. A man of character is one who can make his influence felt among this fellow human being. Most people have no individuality of their own. They are just sharp. They are colourless shadows, without any special mark to distinguish them from others. But a man of character is easily recognized by his behaviour opinions and bearing. All the great men of history were men of character otherwise they would never have achieved name or fame. The first essential of character is moral courage. Moral courage means the courage to face hatred, oppression, criticism for the sake of what we believe to be right. A person who breaks social customs and conventions must have a courage. A girl from an orthodox Hindu family must have fountains of courage before she decides to marry a boy of a low cast. A man of character does not believe in duplicity or diplomacy or achieve an end.

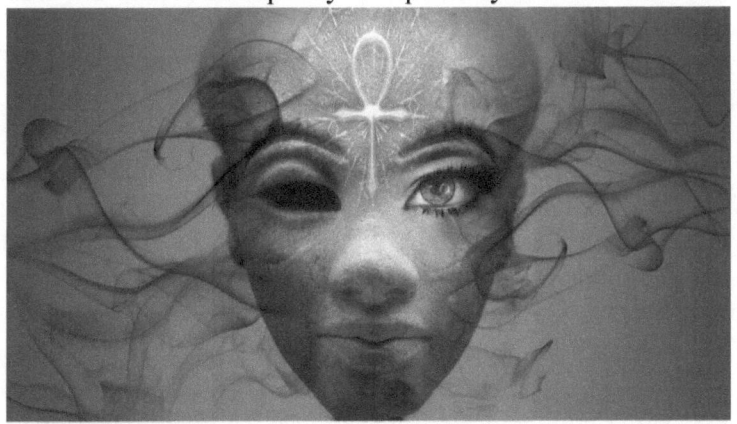

Honestly, loyalty and reliability are important ingredients of character. A man of character does not like corrupt practices. He does not like under-hand means. He fight for right causes he is a believer in justice and fairness. A man with character has firm determination and strong will power. He knows how to carry out his plans without the fear of defeat or disappointment. He does not care of obstacles and difficulties. He is rewarded for his preservation.

Columbus has the firmness of will. He discovered America despite strong opposition from fellow sailors to sail further. Dared Livingstone was also inspired by strong determination of the dark African continent. Another essential feature of character is the capacity to act, to execute, to do things and to give them a practical shape. We may be great idealists. If we lack the will to translate our ideas into action we would be dreamers only.

Character demands a certain faith is one's power. Without this faith, no faith worth the name is possible. Thus character is good combination of several qualities. It is the sum total of moral courage, honesty and integrity, firm determination, capacity for action, consistency and faith in one's ability. All great men of world assessed these qualities in sample measure. Man's fate is pre ordinated by God, and man has no power over his fate. To such, people destiny is character. While many persons believe that man is the maker of his own destiny and fate. A man who wins, is the man, who thinks he can, a man can change his fate, creates his fortune who believes in himself, has positive attitude, strong will, firm determination and zeal to achieve the goals. Character is nothing, but these qualities which shapes the conduct of a person, so character is the real destiny and it is wrong to think that destiny is somewhat a prewritten thing. God also helps those who help themselves. Never design your character like garden where everyone can walk but design your character like to the sky where everyone desire to reach.s

CHAPTER 4

FACE IS THE INDEX OF MIND

———◆———

It is quite true that face is the index of mind. Our thoughts are reflected on our face, when we are afraid of anything, or have a fear of anyone, we turn pale. When angry we grow red-hot. We can judge a person from his face, we can know what may be passing in the mind of a man. His outward smile indicated his real nature. Thoughts and inner feelings are reflected in the mirror of one's face. If you will smile our nature is indicated. Smile is a key towards success. So always smile.

A proverb quotes the face is the index of mind. The people of this age, are always full of anxieties. From the very faces of the people of this age, one can find out the index of the mind. There are sufferings from internal diseases, separation from those near and dear and anxieties for maintaining the status quo.

CHAPTER 5

HONESTY

"Honesty is the first chapter of wisdom"

Honesty is great virtue. It, in fact is the best policy. We should be honest in our word and deeds. It pays a man in the long run. He becomes popular among men and is successful in every walk of life. And honest man may face difficulties in the beginning but ultimately he is rewarded for it.

A dishonest man is always looked down upon and is never trusted by people. We should always be an honest person, honest man is always respected and is rewarded by a great award. He is a man with great honest deeds.

He is honest with parents with friends with everyone. So be honest. Honesty is a best policy.

Honesty help in developing good attributes like kindness, discipline, truthfulness, moral integrity and more. Lying, cheating, lack of trust, steal, greed and other immortal attributes have no part in honesty. Honest people are sincere, trustworthy and loyal throughout their life.

CHAPTER 6

WHERE THERE IS WILL THERE IS WAY

A will finds a way if we are inclined to do thing. We are sure to find a way of doing it. Most of the people think that they cannot do a certain thing only because they have not a strong desire to do it. Most of difficulties are overcome, if we face them boldly. A bad man quarrels with his tools. But a willing worker takes pains for finding a solution to it.

I want to say you short story after reading that you will "where there is will there is way".

It was hot summer day a crow was very thirsty, he flew here and there, in search of water he sat on branch of tree there was pitcher under the tree there was some water in the pitcher he was very happily to see the pitcher. He tried to drink water but the level of water was so low that his peak couldn't reach the water in the pitcher, he thought of plan he dropped some pebbles in the water the level of water rose up, the crow drunk the water and flew away.

"Desire is endless process

Isliya

"Jahan cha wha Rah"

CHAPTER 7

THE PROBLEMS OF UNEMPLOYMENT

---·◆·---

Unemployment is a burning question of the day. It is causing a lot of headache and worry to the government and the people. Educated and qualified young men and women are feeling frustrated because they cannot get jobs. For one post there are hundreds of candidates. Unemployment is causing brain drain because highly qualified doctors, engineers and teachers are leaving India to settle in other countries where they find opportunities of employment.

In India population is increasing at a very rapid speed everyday many thousand babies are born. We welcome every new baby as blessing of God. Sweets are distributed even the birth of twelfth son. A baby that is born today will need and demand a job after twenty years of so. Thus we see that growing population is major factor responsible for employment.

In the modern age woman are the equal of men in every field. They are the rivals of man in the field of employment. They have come out of the four walls of the house, receive education as men do and seek jobs in the same way.

The number of job-seekers has doubled in recent years. Now women work as teachers' clerks, typists, officials and what not. Thus the number of candidates has greatly increased which has resisted in large scale unemployment. Unemployment is not confined to India. It is worldwide phenomenon. All the countries of the world are facing this problem. It is duty of government to give jobs to a man who is willing to work. An idle mind is the devil's workshop. Everyone needs food to eat, clothes to wear and a house to live in freedom and democracy means nothing to those who have nothing to eat. In England and America the government owns it responsibility to provide employment to the people. If it fails to provide employment it pay unemployment allowance. But in India, there is no such provision. It is supposed to be the duty of the citizen to find on seize a job for himself. Favroilism and corruption are in full swing. High jobs are meant for the friends and relatives of high-ups. No problem can be solved by passing laws in parliament. People should also help in the solution of this problem. They must control the growth of population. Young men and women must believe and practice the dignity of labour. They must be ready to work in the field and factories. This is the way of progress, prosperity and happiness.

CHAPTER 8

SCIENCE AND RELIGION

The modern age is the age of science. Scientific discoveries have sounded the death-kneel of religion. In the earlier ages, religion was the prop of life but now science has taken its place. The modern age fights shy of any emotional outbursts accurate scientific judgement.

Mathew Arnold deeply felt the crumbling away of religious beliefs in the world and the increasing hold of doubt on the minds of the people. There was a time when the sea of faith was full to the brain. But there is an ebb-tide in the sea of faith now as unfavourable winds of doubt are blowing in the world. The world has now became barren and men live blindly in ignorance. Christian religion had taught the world that God is all powerful and man was made in the image of God. Man had a soul and it was immoral. The existence of heaven and hell was recognized. But Darwin's theory of the origin of species exploded the myth about man being the direct descendant of Adam and Eve. The faith of man is God was rudely shaken. Science hold that nothing exists outside matter in motion and force. Therefore soul God and heaven are mere myths. Most of the people in the world are convinced by the scientific point of view people in industrialized countries consider in money as their God. They are so busy in earning and spending money that they have no time to think to God.

People in the west are however getting increasingly conscious that man's desires cannot be merely satisfied by food and drink. In moments of difficulty man wants some consolation. Science might have made much progress but it has failed to wipe out spiritualism complexly. People in the east are religious minded.

Pakistan is a theocratic country. The constitution of India makes India a secular country but the people of India are religious minded.

Some people have a wrong thinking they think that there is no difference between the education of science and the education of Islam, by learning the education of science the person will go out of Islam, It is really wrong concept. Also this is determined that scientists are out of Islam. It is wrong, Islam and science are not opposites of each other. They are actually same. By learning the education of science the person can know the world and the secrets of universe. By knowing these things Allah's knowledge is gained and then he admire the mercy of lord. By gaining this knowledge and he shines this knowledge and he lights this knowledge by science.

As per almighty Allah has said that: The most beloved deeds in the sight of Allah are those performed regularly, even if they are less.

"Verily the Almighty is the founder of whole world, the founder of all organism and the founder of skies and lands. The almighty rains rain from sky and grow fruits and vegetables from land and then you eat."

In these verses the almighty highlight that I have made rain and which is rained from sky and I have made land and I growed fruits and vegetables for you. And the water that is present in the rain have lot of fertilizers. Now science will help us and will understand how these fertilizer and present in rain. When the clouds are rumbling and the rain rains and the nitrogen and oxygen which is present in the air mix with each other and by mixing these two nitric oxide are made. Which is present in air and rain make nitric oxide is mixed with air particles and a new fertilizer is made known as Ammonia nitrate. Which is best fertilizer and other particles which are present in rain water are somehow acidic substances and when these acidic substances are fall on land they get mix with land containing substances and when they mix up, a new substance is formed called calcium nitrate which is also best fertilizer.

In this way water which is present in the rain are helpful and best fertilizers are made which are helpful for growth of plants. This is the reason that almighty had made rain water as a resource. The person who didn't understand the education of science will not understand the education of Islam. The education of science is must as of education of Islam. There are also uncountable examples where we see how these two Islam and science are similar.

CHAPTER 9

MAN IS THE SOCIAL ANIMAL

The functions of man and other animals are to a great extent similar. Man has developed brain while other animals do not have such a developed brain. The natural impulses like hunger, thirst, sex and pugnacity are found in all animals a like. Because of the gift of brain possessed by the man, he is superior and created a world of its own developed families, societies, towns, cities, countries man acts and live for the welfare of his family, society. All the actions of the man are oriental for the good causes and for the welfare of the human being while other animals live only for themselves, therefore man is social animal.

CHAPTER 10

WISDOM IS POWER (STORY)

Once there lived an old lion in a forest. He was very cruel. He would kill many animals putting up in that forest. But he would eat only one of the lion, the animals called a meeting. They decided to send one animal daily to the lion. The lion agreed to the proposal. One animal was sent to the lion daily. Many days passed, one day it was the turn of hare. He was clever and fast as compared to others. He thought over a plan. Then has started moving slowly. He reached the lion late in the evening. The lion was sitting in an angry mood. He at once said to the hare "Why are you so late? The hare at once said: It was not my fault, sir I came across another lion on the way. He said that he was the king of all lions he would eat me. He challenged you but I saved myself for you with great difficulty"

The lion once rose up. He became red with anger and said "How does he challenge me." 1 shall see him just now. The wise and clever hare took him to a well. He pointed out that the other lion lived there in the well. The moment the lion peeped into well, he grew angry n seeing his own reflection in the water. He jumped into the well in the feet of anger and was drowned all other animals praised wisdom of the hare. S Greater than bodily Strength" into the will in the fit of anger and was drowned. All other animals praised the wisdom of the hare.

"Wisdom is greater than bodily strength"

CHAPTER 11
EDUCATION

———•♦•———

Education means all round knowledge. Education is the most powerful weapon which we can use to change to world. Education didn't mean to focus on particular subject no. It means to keep knowledge of every field. There is no end of education. It's like deep ocean and how much you have capacity and how much you want learn just learn education of ghosts is education, education of skills is education, education of any subject is education and soon. Everything is education but including knowledge. It is deep topic how much you want know about you can. If you have strong desire to get education and them you will be great educated.

Discipline and dedication is education. A man without behaviour, habits, self-respect is with education. Method of talk, Method of walk is education. You will show-off you ego that really will not lead Education will make you great you will be recognized you success. By education your image will be formed by education. Education is to keep yourself motivate with courage. Train your mind for competitive things.

Education is power is man which cannot borrowed neither stolen. Education is a strength in a person by it you can enlighten the world's history. If we have strong desire, yearn to know we are in search of new things for lighting the world. With the help of knowledge and eeducation a man is turned from beast to great personality, education takes us from darkness to light. At last I would say who so ever have yearning to awake, those who are waiting to be lighted are real future for tomorrow.

CHAPTER 12

PARENTS ARE THE REAL SUCCESS

As far as Allah – Subhana-Wataalah has mentioned in his holy verses "Whoever obeys parents will obey me and whoever disobey parents disobey me"

Parents are the blessing and gift from god they never want bad of us they are always busy in finding happiness and betterment of child. Parent care for us, serve us. They make of future they support us in every field, they want best of their child's, etc so parents are the real strength of world.

Allah has given us life that is only because of our parents. After the obligation of Allah there is obligation of parents, who are real pillars of our life. As far as Allah has said, follow me, follow my rules regulation and all that obey, obey your parents you will succeed in your life.

Your mother nourishes you in her womb with her blood then two years give milk to you, facing all the difficulties all the deadful pain with happiness and joy. We should always be honest with our parents.

If they are old care those them as you can because you are having responsibilities of them. Love them as you can. Parents are the real owner of our life. We should always pray for our parents.

Parents fulfil our all need. We were weak, we can't eat, we can't, write, we can't drink, we can't do any activity only parents helps us at that time they serve us like no other. Now, it out duty if they are old now we should care them, we should not say Ahh! Before them. Today we doctors, we teachers we scientists, al over jobs do us, only because of our parents only because of blessing of them. The father is the door of heaven, and paradise lies beneath of mother. The big personality which are today are because of their parents. Parents are the real success of us. Succession is beneath of parents.

Parents gave us life, they always want good of child. They never have wrong intensions regarding their choms. So, we as the son or daughter of our parents should always respect them. We should love them, we should care them.

We should love our parents

We should care of our parents

We should respect of our parents

We should honour of our parents

And all above, we should serve our parents!!!

CHAPTER 13

LIFE

Life is a four lettered word. To shine with own brightness is life, life of dependence is no life. To have a light of own is life. Life is like a drama where sorrows, sadness, pains, joys and happiness, ups and downs come and go. Life is like chapter where happy and sorrow things happens, we laugh, we cry, we come stand, we stumble all these in life.

Life is to make your name remembered ever. What you want to do, whatever yours desire are bright them, colour them shine them. Beautiful life is life, ugly life is no life. Life is like a new born kid's cries, smiles, angriest etc. that is life.

Make your life masterpiece, image no limitation on what you can be, have or do. Don't be afraid of life. Write your fears and try to overcome them; don't think Big things happens itself it takes sweat, determination, Big personalities become themselves personality "No" There is reason behind every situation. That is "Hard work"

You do, you will go ahead. "Life is Game, play it before you will be outed."

———•♦•———

CHAPTER 14

EDUCATING GIRL MEANS EDUCATING FAMILY

Today's girl child will be the mother of tomorrow, as a mother she can give her child a sound nourishing and capable upbringing. A women has the maximum impact on the social and economic decisions made in family generally. At a micro-level, an educated women helps in making the whole family including the older family members, understand the values and importance of education, and at the micro-level, she adds to the social and economic development of the nation. Girl's education is like sowing the seed which gives rise to green, cheerful and full-grown family plant. In ancient time girls education had a significant place in the society. Gargi and Maiteriya played very encouraging role in spreading the education to the girl extent. The educated girl can shoulder any kind of responsibility. See the examples of Indra Gandhi, Kalpana Chawla, Mother Teresa, Kiran Bedi, Muneeba Mazaira, Miss Mexio in Rosseti, (Miss Universe-2010) Manasvi Mamgai (Miss-India World 2010) and so on. Everyone has earned name in society in our country. An educated women not only helps in nourishing the family in a better, but can help in earning. Napoleon had said

"Give me good mothers and I will give you a great nation."

"Girl is like butterfly then why making them Cry."

Give the girls to fly not the pain to cry & Die.

A Girl Child bring joy, she is no less than a boy.

———————•♦•———————

CHAPTER 15

WORK IS WORSHIP

———•♦•———

We do worship because we want something from the Almighty, in fact it is work, which gives us everything we aspire for. Idless or laziness could not bring us anything. Self-confidence, determination, perseverance and hardwork are the key factors of success. As In case of Shah Faisal (IAS Topper in Kashmir). Whatever invention are seen today are the result of hard work, the will and determination.

The will and the hard work of the inventor found their solution. Impossible is possible for the persons having strong will. In fact impossible is the word which is found the dictionary of fools. Path- of success run through many laby rinth of failure. So it is nothing but hard work that gives us all things we aspire for or we desire or we think of so. "Work is Worship"

CHAPTER 16

A MAN IS KNOWN BY THE COMPANY HE KEEPS

A man is known by the company he keeps is true for all time. This saying is worth its weight in gold. Birds of the same feather flock together. A good man mixed with good people, while a bad man lives in the company he keeps. A single rotten apple spoils the apples if placed a midst them.

If we know the one, we can guess the character of others. If you will get good habits as well as good rules, good deeds to earn. Join good company as of it is important it reflects that. What kind of you are which family you belong and so on.!!!

CHAPTER 17

As YOU SOW, SO SHALL YOU WILL REAP

According to the natural laws every action has equal and opposite reaction. If we plant a sapling of rose or mango we shall have rose and mango. But if we plant cactus we shall have the thorny cactus. It is equally true in the life of an individual or a nation. If a student studies hard in his early life he builds a good career for himself in his youth. Those who neglect studies are not able to secure good jobs. Some turn mafias too and risk their lives.

In the society there is general notion that we cannot makes progress without corrupt practices, parents, tutors, profession, bureaucrats, political leaders all practice immoral ways of life. They place the example of corrupt life before the young ones. It is strong that they expect their children ideal young men and women. They forget that they have sown the seeds of an immoral society. They will have and they have a corrupt society in which idealism has been discarded.

CHAPTER 18

FROM ADAM (A.S.) TO 21ST CENTURY

First person who was sent to earth is Hazrat Adam (A.S.). Many changes come day by day, we see from horse cart to aeroplane, from pigeon's message to text we see great revolution.

Month's journey now in hours that is all wow but behind all the happening there is reason. There is advantage there is disadvantage. Presence of modesty, was there, nothing is present now by following west cultures we forget even though our Soul, we forget our work, we forget our lord, and we forget our saying from our ancestors.

Genesis 5, the book of the generation of Adam, list the descendants of Adam from Seth to Noah with their ages at the birth of their first sons (except Adam himself, for whom his age at the birth of Seth, his third son is given) and their ages at death Adam lives 930 years.

Adam name mentioned in Quran is approximately 25 times. U will find a common word "Inform" them get the Arabic root letter of the word to understand, how Adam is the first Nabi, (Prophet) as well as Khalif (successor) God as told in Quran.

Everybody knows that living in the 21st century offers certain advantages, such as higher standard of living,

But it also has disadvantages, the some depersonalization of human relationships and the weakening of spiritual values. One of the disadvantage which almost all effects that in internet, waste of time. Money frauds, privacy exposure not safe place for children. People often interact with machines then relationships. Due to materialistic culture, people say, faith is science, instead of religion. People need a scientific definition for everything. Few people still accept that Allah, who created everything. However we must make a concerted effort to preserve our both, must is our religion. Moreover, we should take the time now to make our lives more meaningful."

CHAPTER 19

STORY OF WOMEN

―――――♦―――――

This is the story of woman who is perfectly imperfect life made her who, and what is today. It's the story of a woman who in pursuit of her dreams and aspirations made other people realize that if you think that your life is hand and you're giving up on that because you think your life is unfair. Think again. Because when you think that way you being unfair to your own self. It is the story of women who made people realize that sometimes problems are not too big. We are too small because we can't handle them. It is the story of women who we time realized the real happiness doesn't lie in success, money, fame. It lies within real happiness lies in gratitude. So I am going to share that story of women. That is the story of Muniba Mazair's. The story of gratitude. They call it adversity. I (Muniba) call it opportunity. They call it weakness I (Muniba) call it strength. They call her (Muniba) disabled. I (Muniba) call myself (Muniba) differently abled. They see my (Muniba) disability I see my (Muniba) ability. There are some incidents that happens in your life. And those incidents are so strong and they change your DNA. Those incidents or accidents are so strong that they break you physically. They deform your body, but they transform your soul. Those incidents break you.

Deform you but they mold you into the best version of you and the same thing happened to me (Muniba). I (Muniba) was 18 years old when I got married. I (Muniba) belonged to a very conservative family, a Baloch family, where good daughters never say no to their parents. My father wanted me (Muniba) to be married and all I (Muniba) said was if that makes you happy I will (Muniba) say, yes! And of course it was not happy marriage. Just about after two years of getting marriage about nine years ago, I met a car accident somehow her husband fell asleep, and the fell in the ditch. He managed to jump out, saved himself, I (Muniba) am happy for him. But I (Muniba) stayed insided the car. And I sustained a lot of injuries. The list is a bit long. Don't get scared. I (Muniba) am perfectly fine now. Radius Ulna of my right are were fractured. The wrist was fractured. Shoulder and collarbone were fractured, my (Muniba). Who Ribcage got fractured and because of the Ribcage injury. Lungs and liver were badly injured. I (Muniba) couldn't breathe. I (Muniba) lost urinal bowl control and why I (Muniba) have to wear bag wherever, I (Muniba) go, that injury changed me and my life completely as a person in my perception towards living my life. Was the spine injury.

Three vertebrae off my backbone were completely crushed, and I (Muniba) got paralyzed for the rest of my life. So, this accident took place in a far flung area. I (Muniba) was in the middle of nowhere. They dragged me (Muniba) out. Where I realized that words have the power heal the soul and in all that distress and grief somehow or the other those words were so magical that they keep me (Muniba) going. There are always turning points in your life. We all have fear. Fear of unknown, fear of known, fear of losing people, fear of losing help money. We want to excel in a career we want to become famous we want to get money. We are scared all the time. You know that we human beings have a problem out many problems. There is one more, and that is self- created one. We always except ease from life. We have this amazing fantasy about life. This is how things should work. This my plan. It should go as per my plan. If that doesn't happen we give up. This life is a test and trial and test are trials. We you expect ease from life and life gives you lemons then you make lemonade, and then do blame life for that because you were expecting ease from trial. Life is a trial every time you will realize. It's okay to be scared, It's okay to cry, everything is okay, but giving up is not option.

They always say that failure is not an option. Failure should be an option. Because when you will then you get up and that keeps you going and that's how human are strong. We want ourselves to be perfect. There is this image in our head about everything, perfect life, perfect relationships, perfect career, we want everything perfect. Nothing is perfect in this world. In all those imperfections you have to listen to your heart. You don't have to look good for people. 'If your soul is perfect within that is all perfect then)

CHAPTER 20

FAITH

Anything which exists as strength into your body by trusting upon your founder and your belovers. Faith (eman) is explained in different ways as according to belongings. Muslims are known as stronger faithful, as they are capable and having strong faith upon Allah. A person always wants something from Allah, so having faith that there is any power, there is my lord which forward me all the blessing which I see today, which I had seen. Always be thankful to almighty that he creates this world from one being to now this generation. Yes, there is no merciful, no owner, like Allah here and hereafter. This world had to finished, on day it will get vanish, when mountains will break, when sky will break, everyone will find his own ways. Everyone will have fear. No one have see this before, Allah will move this whole earth as he wishes. Mountains will flealike dust. Building, hotels, vilas all destroyed. There will be only the name that is "Allah". We have to prepare ourself for this world and here after. We have to offer 5 prayers, we have to give charity, we have to help the poors as it is our duty. There is another world in which I have faith in which I believe. We have to alive after our death. We have to answer our questions in front of Almighty, we have to stand, we have to stumble, we have to be calm, here grand hereafter. Do pray, do supplication. Supplication is one of the power key. Nothing changes decree (destiny) than supplication. So, supplicate, forget your past make your history. Make your name now. Do great things, "Think great you will have great" Dream big, try to fulfil them. And Allah is there, who is there for helping us in every hard situation "Minor or Major problems doesn't meant by working with beautiful intensions means a lot." (Sabahat)

---

21 CHAPTER

MOTIVATION TO CREATE LIFE

How can a man create his life?

How will this life be beautiful?

Which way can life be beautiful?

If you want to build life well

Then it will be necessary to think better. You can enlighten your future by achieving the goal of life. Work as hard as possible to reach your goals. There are many people around you who have a lot at the top level. Those who have left on a bright future.

How did they make their lives so beautiful? Why cannot you? You can research about their past. You will know how hard they are at this stage you can also go to a good level if you want.

For this you have to do:

1) You have to find a goal in your life. It is good to set goals of night in student life. If you are not a student you will find Life's goals. If you do not study you will be able to succeed and get into a good level.

2) Keep your self-confidence.

3) Make yourself ready to work hard.

4) You must love your profession.

5) Leave laziness and be brave.

The motivation for future plans

The future plan is very important. For a young man. To make future chats through the job or business. There is also a plan for what is going on for the future people have to face many problem of the plan is not good. This may break the hope of success. So should be well planned.

How to plan

1) To find out the purpose of life to set the future.

2) A goal will be to decide on life.

3) The whole plan will be in matching with yourself. So that's what you like to do.

4) Try to finish the difficult task first

By doing such plans, we can make our future better. This requires motivation. People have many problems while planning the future. Have the confidence to solve all these problems. You must be self-confident.

Motivation for success:

Must be successful in life. You have to build your own career. We will succeed one after the other. Failed life is very difficult a successful life is the most beautiful.

Actually, we need motivation for what we want to succeed. That may be the case of our studies, jobs, business, relations, record etc.

Must have to work loved to achieve success, no matter what works. You must love your profession. Do not say give up. Find out the time for your profession. Keep in mind that, in exchange for anything, you have to achieve success. Work in the right way. If you do this then you will succeed.

Motivation for job and business

Young people need to be e serious about work because we have to be something to survive in life. After completing the study, you have to spend life in business or in a job. Then you will think that your life has been set. But in these cases the motivation is important.

1) Love your profession. Whether it's job or business small or big.

2) Work as hard as you can.

3) Never say "I cannot do this" don't worry, everything is possible for you. Nothing seems impossible.

4) If you cannot improve in the business or the job, then do not give up, Be confident that you can.

5) Do not think of yourself alone

6) Do not feel weak or disabled yourself.

7) Think life is Battleground, and you are the soldier. You must win the war.

8) These are some business related motivations.

Some motivations for young people in the field of education:

1) Find out how to enjoy your studies.

2) Think you have done good results in the exam. Then how much pleasure you will feel!

How happy your parents will be! Think of those days, of course, you can study well.

3) The first thing you find most difficult is to finish it first.

4) Leave the things that compel you to study.

5) Relate to good students.

6) Research on study topics.

7) Most of the time try to spend to study.

8) If try this, I hope that good student can get good results. This is the motivation for the education of youth.

Motivation to increase self confidence

How do you boost your self-confidence? There will be nothing with confidence. All work requires self-confidence. Such thinking proves to be the weakness of the human kind. There is more, it is...."I do

Not know what I can do. The head is not working. I do not understand what to do etc."

When do people say such a thing?

When people are in confusion.

And people cannot make any discussion for the confusion. If you can overcome this confusion people's confidence will increase. The youth must be confident. It's a wonderful inspiration for you in the subject of motivational topics for youth. That will spell your confidence.

22 CHAPTER

SAY 'NO' TO DRUGS

———•♦•———

Drugs are chemical that change the way a person's body works. Many people around the world are mostly seeking help of this drugs medicine to relieve themselves from suffering, feelings of loneliness, stress, unhappy relationship and get high while seldom do they realize for this momentary pleasures they are putting their lives and stakes. This offer leads to drug abuse and addiction which is a serious issue. Drugs harm our physical mental and emotional well-being in many ways. They make you irritable, aggressive, intolerant, addictive, and overly stimulated. Also causes infection possible heart failure, insomnia, depression, high blood pressure etc. People even after knowing its side effects tend to 'try' them and fall into addiction eventually. Add more about the drugs and how it is proving to be a great threat to people especially teenagers who fall prey to it mostly. I suggest you to do some research on drugs (i.e. like mariguana, LSD, heroine, morphine). So be away from the things.

DRUGS WILL HAUNT YOU FOR

LIFE, SO SAY NO TO

DRUGS!

OH MY GOD, OH MY GOD,

Oh my God, oh my God,
You are my lord, you are my lord,
You gave me worth
You sent me on earth
You are the one who make the world
You are the one who break the world,
Oh my God, you are my lord,
You make scenery,
You make greenery
You make mountains
You make fountains
Oh my God
You are my lord
Give me feel
To achieve the Zeal
Give me power
To face the trial
Oh my God,

You are my lord,
Make me shine day by day
guide me Allah towards your way
Oh My God
You are My Lord.

ALLAH

Oh Allah you are the God
Oh Allah you are the lord,
Everything is in front of you,
Your nature is unique,
In leaves there is greenery
In roses there is Redness,
Every work is done by you
Your name is unique
This earth is fire and water
This is your pity
Large mountains are quite infront of you.
You name is special
Oh Allah, you are God,
You are lord,

SIN

Whole world is buzy
In enjoying there lives
Doing sins day and night
Without any fear or tense
Holding wine in their hands
Drinking it as sharbat
Spending time in parties, like
Spending time in Salaat,
Making list of bears
Like writing philosophy
Doing sins day and night
They will surely know about it they will find the way,
But after going time
Realizing their bad deeds But after going time
Men is imitating women.
People are treating relatives badly,
Interest is becoming an art.
People are leaving prayers.
May Allah show us great path.
Sin, Sin, Sin, Don't Do Sin.

23 CHAPTER

ALLAMA IQBAL

———•———

Sir Muhammad allama Iqbal was a South Asian writer, philosopher ,and politician whose poetry in the Urdu language is thought by many to be among the greatest of the twentieth century and whose version of a cultural and political ideal for the Muslims of British ruled India was to animate the impulse for pakistan.he was born in Sialkot Pakistan.

Allama Iqbal is my inspiration and I can say foundation of my book . without allama's poetry it wasn't possible to pen down a single letter.most people are so busy trying to get somewhere else they never stop and appreciate the miracle all around them .they never stop and appreciate the magic of journey.he inspired me by his poetry collection about life , study and Islam in Urdu ."Amal sa Zindagi Banti hai janat bhi ,jahanam bhi ,ya khaki apni fitrat mein na noori hai na naari hai ...

Switch your mentality for "i m broken and helpless"to I m growing and healing and watch how your life change for the better.

The golden words from book Bali jibraeal of allama Iqbal that changed my life :

Man ki duniya ,man ki duniya suuz_o _ masti zajbo shook ,tan ki duniya ,tan ki duniya,suudo_sooda makro fan : world soul the world of fire and ecstasy and longing world of sense ,the world of gain that fraud and cunning blight ...

Man ki dawlat haath ati Hain to phir jaati nhi ,tan ki dawlat Chaw hai ata hai Dan jaata hai dann : treasure of the soul once won is never lost again , treasure gold ,a Shadow _wealth soon comes and soon takes flight ..

Man ki duniya maana paya mana afrangi Ka raaj ,man ki duniya ma na dakhaa ma naa sheikho barhaman: in the spirit's world I have not seen a white man's Raj,in that world I have not seen hindu and Muslim fight ....

,Pani Pani kargayi muj ko kalander ki ya baath ,tu juka jab ghaar Ka aaga na maan Tara na man :shame and shame that hermit's saying pouted on me you forfeit body and soul alike if once you cringe to another's might...

Apna man ma doob kar paaja suraga Zindagi Tu agr mara nhi banta na ban apna to ban: delve into your soul and there seek our life's buried tracks; will you not be mine ? Then be not mine , be your own right!!

And yes,that transform my soul .they always say time changes things,but you actually have to change them yourself ..if you want to fly,give up everything that weights you down!!!

www.ingramcontent.com/pod-product-compliance
Lightning Source LLC
LaVergne TN
LVHW041552070526
838199LV00046B/1931